Everyone
Eats

Nancy Kelly Allen

rourkeeducationalmedia.com

*Scan for Related Titles
and Teacher Resources*

Teaching Focus:

Phonics: Concepts of Print- Have students find capital letters and punctuation in a sentence. Ask students to explain the purpose for using them in a sentence.

Before Reading:

Building Academic Vocabulary and Background Knowledge

Before reading a book, it is important to set the stage for your child or students by using pre-reading strategies. This will help them develop their vocabulary, increase their reading comprehension, and make connections across the curriculum.

1. *Read the title and look at the cover. Let's make predictions about what this book will be about.*
2. *Take a picture walk by talking about the pictures/photographs in the book. Implant the vocabulary as you take the picture walk. Be sure to talk about the text features such as headings, Table of Contents, glossary, bolded words, captions, charts/ diagrams, or Index.*
3. Have students read the first page of text with you then have students read the remaining text.
4. *Strategy Talk – use to assist students while reading.*
   - *Get your mouth ready*
   - *Look at the picture*
   - *Think…does it make sense*
   - *Think…does it look right*
   - *Think…does it sound right*
   - *Chunk it – by looking for a part you know*
5. *Read it again.*
6. *After reading the book complete the activities below.*

Content Area Vocabulary
Use glossary words in a sentence.

caterpillars
chopsticks
sushi
tarantula
tortillas
utensil

After Reading:

Comprehension and Extension Activity

After reading the book, work on the following questions with your child or students in order to check their level of reading comprehension and content mastery.

1. *Can you eat foods from different countries in the United States? Explain. (Text to self connection)*
2. *Why are some foods more popular in other countries? (Asking questions)*
3. *What are your favorite foods? (Text to self connection)*
4. *What is common among all the countries in the book? (Summarize)*

Extension Activity

Try something new! With an adult, search for a recipe from another country. When you find something you want to try have an adult help you make the food. How was it? What does it taste like? When would you eat this food? Share your experience with your family or classmates through a presentation.

Would you eat a bug?

In the United States, people don't usually eat bugs.

Spider

Caterpillar

Around the world, many people eat
spiders and **caterpillars**.

In Cambodia, people enjoy a crunchy snack made of fried **tarantula**.

In South Africa, caterpillars are cooked in a stew.

Pizza is a favorite food for many people.

Italy is famous for pizza, but people in Norway eat the most of it!

Much of the food in Japan is only lightly cooked.

Sushi is a Japanese meal made with raw fish.

Rice and corn feed people around the world.

In India, rice is made into pancakes.

In the United States, rice and corn are used to make cereal.

In Mexico, **tortillas** are made from corn.

Do you like chocolate? People in Switzerland eat the most.

Vanilla ice cream is popular all over the world.

People in Australia eat the most ice cream.

Many people eat with a fork or spoon.
In China, Korea, and Japan, people eat
with **chopsticks**.

In India, some people use their right hand
as an eating **utensil**.

Oysters

Cod

In places near water, many people eat seafood. Salmon and oysters are favorites in Ireland.

On the island of Jamaica, people eat cod, also called saltfish, and curried goat.

So many bananas are grown in Uganda, the people there eat them almost every day.

Pasta might be the world's favorite food! People in Poland enjoy pierogies.

People in China make birthday noodles instead of cake.

Around the world, people eat some foods that we eat. They also eat different foods. What we eat tells a lot about who we are and where we live. What's for dinner?

Photo Glossary

 **caterpillars** (KAT-ur-pil-urs): The larva of a butterfly or moth.

 **chopsticks** (CHAHP-stiks): Thin sticks used to eat food.

 **sushi** (soo-shee): Small cakes of cooked rice with raw fish or vegetables wrapped in seaweed.

 **tarantula** (tuh-RAN-chuh-luh): A large, hairy spider.

 **tortillas** (tor-TEE-yuhs): A round, flat bread made from cornmeal or flour.

 **utensil** (yoo-TEN-suhl): A tool used to eat food.

Index

Show What You Know

1. Why do people eat different foods in different countries?
2. What are some foods that people around the world eat?
3. What are some unusual foods people eat?

Websites to Visit

pbskids.org/arthur/games/lunchomatic/lunchomatic.html

www.zisboombah.com/pickchow

www.funbrain.com/brain/JustForFunBrain/Games/Game.html?GameName=DontGrossOutTheWorld

About the Author

Nancy Kelly Allen lives in Kentucky. When she was a little girl, she made mud pies of dirt and water. One day, she tasted one. Once was enough. Today, when she eats the mud pies, they are made of cookies, fudge sauce, and ice cream.

Meet The Author!
www.meetREMauthors.com

© 2016 Rourke Educational Media

www.rourkeeducationalmedia.com

PHOTO CREDITS: Cover: © KPG Payless2, Wiktory; Page 1: © Karelnoppe; Page 3: © Loretta Hostettler; Page 4: © ildogesto, Artistic Captures; Page 5: © CrackerClips, ByronD; Page 6: © Peter Stuckings; Page 7: © ComQuat-Wikipedia; Page 8: © Stokpro; Page 9: © UlygarGeographic; Page 10: © TAGSTOCK1; Page 11: © Junghee Choi; Page 12: maayeka; Page 13: © ola-p, fcafotodigital; Page 14: © Martinan; Page 15: © Squaredpixels; Page 16: © FangXiaNuo; Page 17: © szefei; Page 18: © Floortje, alexsalcedo; Page 19: © Goddard-Photography; Page 20: © bhofackz, GMVozd; Page 21: © monkeybusinessimages

Edited by: Keli Sipperley

Cover and Interior design by: Tara Raymo

Library of Congress PCN Data

Everyone Eats / Nancy Kelly Allen

(Little World Everyone Everywhere)

ISBN (hard cover)(alk. paper) 978-1-63430-363-7

ISBN (soft cover) 978-1-63430-463-4

ISBN (e-Book) 978-1-63430-560-0

Library of Congress Control Number: 2015931700

Printed in the United States of America, North Mankato, Minnesota

Also Available as:

ROURKE'S
e-Books